Give Me Your Hand

Among Paul Durcan's other books are

The Berlin Wall Café
Going Home To Russia
Daddy, Daddy
Crazy About Women
A Snail In My Prime

Give Me Your Hand

Poems by

PAUL DURCAN

MACMILLAN
LONDON
published in association with
NATIONAL GALLERY PUBLICATIONS, LONDON

First published 1994 by Macmillan London Limited
a division of Pan Macmillan Publishers Limited
Cavaye Place London SW10 9PG
and Basingstoke

Associated companies throughout the world

ISBN 0-333-58593-3

1 3 5 7 9 8 6 4 2

A CIP catalogue record for this book is available from
the British Library

Photoset by Parker Typesetting Service, Leicester

Printed and bound in Great Britain by
Butler & Tanner Ltd, Frome and London

to

Harriet Waugh

Painting is not my life. My life is my life.

R. B. Kitaj

CONTENTS

INTRODUCTION

I have a passion for the truth and for the fictions that it authorizes.
JULES RENARD, *Journals*

IN USING paintings as a point of departure for so many of his poems – and often travelling without a ticket, from the viewpoint of a sober art historian – Paul Durcan forges a strong personal link with a fascinating sequence of encounters between poets and painters. It started in modern times loosely speaking, with Baudelaire, although *Les Phares*, of course, which first appeared in 1857 in *Les Fleurs du Mal*, is a sequence of invocations to individual artists or reflections on them – Rubens, Leonardo, Rembrandt, Michelangelo, Puget, Watteau, Goya and Delacroix. The robustly operatic fulsomeness of Baudelaire's exhortations is quite different to Aretino's searching lines on Titian nearly three hundred years earlier. At a negative extreme, in Sartre's *La Nausée*, the protagonist's first sensation of alienation, of an existentialist view of life, comes from contact with a painting in the Uffizi.

Poetry changes but the challenge of art for poetry has long and quite ancient roots: poets have often addressed or dedicated poems to painters and sculptors or made images with words to reflect the visual or even moral world. Durcan has been doing this for many years but in this collection of poems he has for the second time taken his inspiration from individual paintings in a public collection.

Durcan does much more than extend an interesting tradition, for these beautiful and constantly surprising poems have poetic self-sufficiency and keep the paintings firmly in their place. They are not concerned with the description or interpretation that our sober art historian could provide. Often the tone is elegiac.

We don't read Paul Durcan to have a picture's content or message handed to us but to add another dimension, a fresh image to our sense of life. Enjoying Durcan as I do, I should be just as happy to read poems inspired by a take-away or a pair of old trousers but in this book he uses paintings with characteristic insight – and poetic licence. Often the poem makes us think again about a cherished painting.

Durcan's poetry is so full of life, so artful in its vernacular ease, its formal simplicity; the poet is always right there, in life, with you: he doesn't set poetry up on a pedestal – and yet how imaginatively vivid and alert his lines can be.

Durcan has delightful but sometimes abrasive things to tell us in an odd double-take of memory and ideas. Irony is as near as he gets to indictment. The unselfconscious, everyday beauty of his command of language, the clarity of his tone of voice, ensure attention and make a claim on our memory. He speaks with the autobiographical, circumstantial assurance of the sophisticated provincial, as in Joyce, in Beckett or in Svevo. In Irish poetry, which seems more fully alive, certainly fresher than English poetry these days, the poetry of Paul Durcan stands out with its strong character.

Although I have lived all my life through my eyes – in looking at art, making exhibitions, persuading artists to design for the stage, and writing or talking about art – the word for me comes first. This is not to say that words precede images for, in my mind, they are inseparable. But art has always appeared to me as a fantastic extension of life whereas poetry seems like the most fundamentally considered response. For this reason, I am a slow reader of poetry, approaching it warily as if it were some exotic plant in the everyday thickets of common exchange. The only reason for this lapse into self-explanation is because in writing about Paul Durcan I am straying considerably beyond my usual patch of turf; on such an occasion there is an urge to explain oneself or to claim an alibi.

Durcan has often read his poems in London but we have never met or had any contact. The invitation to write this note for his book came out of the blue from the poet, via his publishers, but it is not surprising in a way, for life is filled with coincidence and convergence. Not long ago, after wanting for years to read the difficult poetry of Celan, I found at last piles of books by this writer in a bookshop in Paris. I bought a couple and began to read. That night I went to a dinner party given by a great friend and sat opposite a charming elderly woman whose name escaped me. Next day, telling my hostess of my pleasure at reading Celan at last, she told me that I had been sitting opposite his widow at dinner.

In writing about paintings Durcan is in interesting company. After Baudelaire, Rilke wrote some poems in this genre and Lorca wrote at least one poem about the dream world of Salvador Dali, with whom he was painfully in love. Rafael Alberti wrote vividly and most sensuously about Picasso. There are many Russian poems about paintings, beginning with Mayakovsky. Octavio Paz has written numerous poems about paintings and there is the great collaboration over several years in the late sixties between Paz and Robert Motherwell: *A la Pintura*. It was Motherwell who once defined for me the essence of modernity, its crucial element, as 'the freedom from nostalgia'. If you think of Matisse and Brancusi, you know that Motherwell was right. Durcan's poetry for all its strong feeling, sense of exact incident, place and time, is free of nostalgia.

Among several American poets who have written about paintings, either incidentally in poems or in poems on specific works of art addressed to artists, Frank O'Hara was the closest in friendship and in critical appreciation to a number of outstanding painters and sculptors in the USA. He wrote several poems for the painter Larry Rivers, his great friend and occasional lover. John Ashbery has used art and artists as themes. Marianne Moore wrote amusingly as ever about buying a painting, and William Carlos Williams wrote about Bruegel's *The Fall of Icarus*; and so did W. H. Auden in *Musée des Beaux Arts*.

Yeats wrote about Dulac's *Black Centaur*; Edith Sitwell wrote several poems about the fantastic world of her unresponsive beloved, Pavel Tchelitchev, and David Gascoyne, during and after his association with surrealism, has also written about painting. W. S. Graham wrote an elegy for Peter Lanyon after that artist's tragic early death in a gliding accident. Charles Tomlinson has meditated on John Constable; Derek Mahon's poem about Uccello's *The Hunt by Moonlight* and Eavan Boland on Degas's *Laundresses* extend the genre. A poem from George Barker was commissioned for the catalogue of Robert Colquhoun's retrospective exhibition at the Whitechapel Gallery in 1958, and Thomas Blackburn wrote for Arthur Boyd's catalogue for his Whitechapel show in 1963.

Not surprisingly French poetry provides us with the greatest variety of encounters starting, after Baudelaire, with Apollinaire's poem about Picasso's *Saltimbanques* and then *Les Fenêtres*, the poem that conjures up the new multi-faceted vision of cubism. Max Jacob, who taught the young Picasso how to speak French correctly, wrote poems about his much loved pupil.

Cocteau also wrote poems about Picasso and other contemporaries. Blaise Cendrars wrote the *Transsibérien* prose poem which Sonia Delaunay decorated so memorably as a collaboration. Beginning with André Breton, the surrealists wrote copiously on paintings and painters from Tristan Tzara and Philippe Soupault to Aragon and Eluard. René Char composed some of the most brilliant and sharply pitched of all the surrealist poems.

Eluard wrote often about paintings and collaborated with Marc Chagall in a lovely edition printed just after the 1939–45 war of his sequence of poems *Le Dur Désir de Dürer*. St Jean Perse wrote a startlingly fresh and urgent poem on the theme of *Les Oiseaux* of Georges Braque. Arp, of course, wrote his own poetry as often as he made sculpture and paintings. As well as interpreting the work of the van de Velde brothers, Jack Yeats and his wartime companion in France, Henri Hayden, Beckett peopled all his works with recapitulations of his encounters with great European paintings that he had spent decades studying as he travelled in Europe in the twenties and thirties. Echoes of paintings, an eye here, a hand there, are interwoven through all his work.

Durcan is in a category of his own in the ease and sleight-of-hand with which he glides in and out of the subject or content of each painting that inspires him. He projects himself into the personages, the situations; imagines a development in the action, treats the paintings like kites in the gusty air of his imagination. This is not new for Durcan, who takes on as many roles as sexes in much earlier poetry.

He has been ascribing poems to artists for many years, beginning with Rembrandt for *The Jewish Bride*, and in 1991 he produced a whole book of new poems, *Crazy About Women*, on paintings in the National Gallery of Ireland. In his Preface to that collection, Durcan describes how the origins of his love for painting, which he shares with an equivalent passion for the images of cinema, came from visits with his mother to Sheila Fitzgerald, a painter who gave classes in her home in Dublin. Later, working in London as a clerk for the North Thames Gas Board, adjacent to the Tate Gallery, he walked out every lunch-time through the back gate 'under a billboard proclaiming "*Look Ahead with Gas*" to sit in front of the pictures of Francis Bacon. These pictures lit up the gloom of life and turned my eyesight inside out.' In 1980, Durcan visited R. B. Kitaj's *The Artist's Eye* show at the National Gallery and this expanded Durcan's approach to art, 'revolutionized it and gave me back the authority of my own eyes'. Durcan's authority is our wonder.

BRYAN ROBERTSON

Give Me Your Hand

THE MARRIAGE OF THE VIRGIN
Niccolò di Buonaccorso

THE MARRIAGE OF THE VIRGIN

As Joseph is thirty years older than me
I am giving him my hand, giving him
The benefit of the doubt under my palm tree.
Isn't he a dote in his bare feet!
I come to him abstract as an abstract carpet!

Since we cannot have a child of our own
We are adopting the child on the edge of the picture,
Far off away out down there on the marble,
The little boy engrossed in the bongos.
He will be our very own dove and although

In the end the hawks will get him
We will build for him a dovecote of his own
Whence he can fly hither, thither as he pleases
With other doves and if he transpires to be gay
We will love him every bit as much if not more.

I will frame our wedding portrait
For him to hang from his balcony and gaze at
The night before they kidnap him in Jerusalem.
Joseph says that the Neighbours will kidnap him.
I love Joseph because he is not afraid of the Neighbours.

He blows his own trumpet in front of the Neighbours.
He does not kowtow to the Neighbours.
He does not pay protection money to the Neighbours.
He does not skip to the tune of the Neighbours.
Poor Old Joe! He chooses his own music!

The Arnolfini Marriage
Jan van Eyck

THE ARNOLFINI MARRIAGE

We are the Arnolfinis.
Do not think you may invade
Our privacy because you may not.

We are standing to our portrait,
The most erotic portrait ever made,
Because we have faith in the artist

To do justice to the plurality,
Fertility, domesticity, barefootedness
Of a man and a woman saying 'we':

To do justice to our bed
As being our most necessary furniture;
To do justice to our life as a reflection.

Our brains spill out upon the floor
And the terrier at our feet sniffs
The minutiae of our magnitude.

The most relaxing word in our vocabulary is 'we'.
Imagine being able to say 'we'.
Most people are in no position to say 'we'.

Are you? Who eat alone? Sleep alone?
And at dawn cycle to work
With an Alsatian shepherd dog tied to your handlebars?

We will pause now for the Angelus.
Here you have it:
The two halves of the coconut.

AN UNIDENTIFIED SCENE

Auditioning in Trafalgar Square at dawn
Under the eye of Nelson,
The hills of south London on the skyline,
The other girls and I are appalled
To be confronted by a pair of critics
On the steps of the National Gallery
But we do not panic, we do not confuse
Our horizontals with our verticals, we do not turn
And flee down the Strand, stumbling
Across traffic islands and zebra crossings.
We continue singing to the gods,

AN UNIDENTIFIED SCENE
Domenico Beccafumi

Sauntering to our destinies,
In Wembley or in Birkenau,
Taking no notice
Of judges, geneticists, critics.

Ladies and Gentlemen – we present
The Apocalypse of John –
A film by Beccafumi.

Afterwards in our dressing rooms in Shaftesbury Avenue
Washing out our knickers,
Chatting to our monkeys,
Disposing of panty liners,
We all fall silent as we stare
At the sole tree.
All break out in sobbing,
Small smoky sobs.
Have one – go on, do – just one.
Just one small smoky sob for you from me.
From an actress you once savaged in Trafalgar Square.
You will carry my shadow around in your arms
For the remainder of your days.

Look, here God does not live among human beings.
The world of the past has not gone.

Apollo and Daphne
Antonio del Pollaiuolo

APOLLO AND DAPHNE

I am a white-haired evergreen in Ladbroke Grove
Keeping Paddy Happy.

In Granny's cottage
High above the Thames
One night when Granny was away
When he rugby-tackled me in his amatory way
Not seeming to know my valley from my mountain
He did not activate my hackles.
He cried: I want to cavort.
I smiled: Not having.

A man cannot take root.
Cannot live on water alone.
Or is it that a woman has in her
A self-sufficient photosynthesis –
A simple acceptance of being a tree?
A recognition – a song or a dance –
That every woman is a tree in winter.
That human beings are primal trees.

Now I am an elderly nymph pale
And interesting in my own
Granny cottage above the Thames
Not resting on my laurels
But having to dance with a zealous,
Bald, self-engrossed, drunk, little paranoid.
Totally off his rocker, poor boy.
'I want to cavort.' 'Not having.'

I am a white-haired evergreen in Ladbroke Grove
Keeping Paddy Happy.

The Virgin and Child with Saints Anthony Abbot and George
Pisanello

THE VIRGIN AND CHILD WITH SAINTS ANTHONY ABBOT AND GEORGE

I am a curly-headed, cocky, moody, young stockbroker,
A Goldilocks barely out of my teens,
Boy George the Twenty-Third.
What I live for
Is my new sports car,
An Alfa Romeo
With a brace of fillies,
A red and a grey,
Cresting my bonnet.
I fancy myself.
I do not aim to stick around for the Flood.

On Sunday mornings
I drive down the sticks
To click with my chick:
Tog out in my lingerie,
Don my boots, my pads, my spurs,
My skirts, my stays, my pins,
My necklaces, my gauntlets, my breastplates,
My wide-brimmed filigree straw hat
With its single white feather bequeathed me
By my mother before she skipped
Out of this world with Motor Neurone Disease.

Soon as I step down out of my bubble
Her father – the horrible hermit –
Is waiting to eat me,
The flood-eroded pavement disintegrating under our feet.
He is forever sounding me out
With a stethoscope masquerading as a bell.
Still, we get along well enough.
A pair of right cads.
His hog lies down on the floor
With my dragon
While we watch the Olympics on TV.

Am I worthy of his daughter?
I can hear him grunting
As yet another gold discus
Hurtles through the screen.
All I can grunt
Is that I like her quite awfully
And she washes my silk socks
And she irons my silk shirts
And she takes no bullshit from me
Be it golden bullshit
Or be it not golden bullshit.

I am a kinky stockbroker, sceptical, cruel.
When I am not thinking of her
Or of my new car
I am thinking of my mother
Skipping out of Motor Neurone Disease.
It jigged all through her body,
A scenic sort of sunny halo with serrated edges
Weaving its blue coastlines in and out
Her hands, her feet, her mountains, her islands.
Who invented my mother?
Packaged her as a Celtic Madonna?

At nightfall I go out to the edge of the fairy wood
To feed my new car;
The fairy wood where in the Deluge I will hide
All my Ernsts, all my Magrittes, all my Warhols.
O Mother.
I do quite awfully like her. But.
Something in the curtain – behind it.
Something in the sea – under the wave.
Something in the bed – under the sheet.
Why do little boys
Jilt their mummies?

SAINT JOHN THE BAPTIST RETIRING TO THE DESERT

I am the Bradford Baptist Saint David Hockney
Retiring into the desert above Los Angeles
For my self-portrait of the artist as a middle-aged mystic;
Between bouquets I go for long drives in my Estate
When nobody interrupts and I can concentrate.
Now you miss me, now you don't miss me.

SAINT JOHN THE BAPTIST RETIRING TO THE DESERT
Giovanni di Paolo

THE PRESENTATION IN THE TEMPLE

I was a middle-aged playwright in London going nowhere
When on a grey Saturday afternoon in January
I wandered into Westminster Cathedral – a home
From home – its black unfinished domes
A source of consolation. In the bosom of Abraham,
I feel, sitting under them, imploring God's mercy,
I who had flown into a rage the previous night in a Battersea pub
Because my poor wife had worn her green frock with a slit in it.

There was a little ceremony in progress in a side-chapel.
Father Simeon, an old Jesuit I've known for years,
Decent skin, camping it up on the altar
But in the most touching way you can imagine.
A young couple presenting to him their baby son,
The manic-depressive husband fishing in his purse for money.
That was the moment of my alteration,
My copping-on to myself, my epiphany.

Bareheaded in the background with my hat in my hands
I says to myself: Enough of all this old self-pity.
Enough of groaning under the weight of the world
Like them two little black lads under the altar.
I've got as pretty a pair of feet as any male playwright
In Great Britain and Ireland – time I made use of them.
Flaunt what you have – as the girl said.
(From Tasmania, she was. Hobart. Sue.)

The Presentation in the Temple
The Master of the Life of the Virgin

Look at Simeon – the care with which
He's holding up that child – the effort of affection he's putting
Into the whole simple little mundane transaction.
Sexy is not a word you'd properly associate with Simeon
But today it's the only word, the right word, the procreative word.
Just look at that bit of ankle he's showing.
From knee to spine he's all ankle.
That's what living in the here and now does for you.

Enough of living in the past – all stabbings and drunkenness,
Father and son, brother and brother, prophet and prophet,
Old hat.
From this day on – this grey January afternoon
I am going to take in my hands
The child of the future
And my tuning fork will be his spiky halo.
I'll have two plays running simultaneously in the West End

And me and Father Simeon will take a holiday in Spain
On the proceeds – why not?
It's a matter of hands but it's also a matter of feet.
Look down at your own feet and think for a moment:
Think of all the men you know who have women's feet.
Next time you are walking down the Charing Cross Road
Look up at my name in red neon lights:
My *nom de plume* – 'The Master of the Life of the Virgin'.

Portrait of a Lady in Yellow
Alesso Baldovinetti

PORTRAIT OF A LADY IN YELLOW

I

I fly over to London
– British Midland Diamond Service –
To identify her remains.

She is laid out on her side
In profile
On a lapis lazuli blue cloth
In a gold casket.

An incendiary device
In a bookshop
On the Charing Cross Road;
A confused phone warning
In I.R.A. code;
You who loved your native land
Of Ireland and books.

II

O my daughter
Of the three palm trees
Give me your hand.
Your singing neck.

Your thinking nose.
Your hatted eye.
Your dab eyebrow.
Your maybe-will-I-never-laugh-again mouth.
Your plaits.
Your shaven soul.

You for whom Sinéad O'Connor
Is a modern heroine;
You for whom Sinéad O'Connor
Is a point of honour.

III

While you were alive
I used scribble notes
To you and tear them up.
Notes that all said
'I miss you.'

O my daughter.
My mandolin in the window.
My bedroom door.
My ikon.
My handkerchief under my pillow.
My snake.
Three feminine vowels.
I miss you.

SAMSON AND DELILAH
Andrea Mantegna

SAMSON AND DELILAH I

I

Pity about Samson.
I love him.

But let me be not sentimental.
He got what he wanted–

Got to die in my arms,
Making love to me.

What every Samson yearns for–
To die in his Delilah's arms.

A man can have
One hangover too many.

My poor old ram
Expiring in my clutches.

The nape of his neck.
I'd know that nape anywhere.

Only the waters of life can save him–
Of the next life.

II

On my milking stool
Under the grape tree

I am a cellist
Playing my man.

My knees wide apart,
A furore of stillness.

A red sky at night
Is a shepherd's delight.

Black stars
In a red night.

When I am done playing
My little man

I hold him over the trough
While he gulps his gulp.

A woman's task is to learn her man
The reality of the resurrection.

Pity about men
All the time pining to die.

CHARLEMAGNE AND THE MEETING OF SAINTS JOACHIM AND ANN AT THE GOLDEN GATE

You have all heard of Charlemagne.
You might not know much about him
But you do know that he was the Boss.
I was his weekend lover for years
But I have no beans to spill.
Glad to disappoint the hacks.
He was always most courtly to women.
Many is the black summer Sunday I happily
Spent with him in the Jerusalem Hilton.
I can see him now sitting up at the bar
Sipping his consommé and vodka
In his red toupee and false beard
Before we'd retire for the afternoon to his suite.
After our dalliance – which I never wholly enjoyed
Although it was all right – it could have been worse –
Intercourse is simply not what it's cracked up to be –
The best part was Charlie taking off his gear
Or trying to take off his gear –
All those shinguards, spurs, kneepads,
Thigh-shields, garters, stays –
After it, we'd troop up the winding stair
– Our ritual family Sunday afternoon outing –
Up onto the battlements where while he'd gaze
Into his crystal ball, I'd gaze down at the swans,
A pair of swans down below in the moat.
I yearn to be a pen with a cob of my own.
I never want to have to have an abortion.

Charlemagne and the Meeting of Saints Joachim and Ann
Studio of the Master of Moulins

It happened just like that.
At the Golden Gate – of all places.
A common or garden proletarian –
Joachim was his name –
I'd often noticed him playing cricket –
A little wicketkeeper, a little bat –
Stopped me and he stared, peered,
Owlwise into my eyes and the way he said to me
'I want to be your husband'
I could feel him husbanding me.
I knew then in that moment –
In that all-conceiving moment –
That I never again wanted to be Charlie's lover.
(No disrespect to Charlie.)
More than anything on heaven or earth
I wanted to be husbanded
And to live in a world beyond sex
And power, beyond all abortion;
To dwell in a dandelion world.
Charlemagne didn't mind –
There were lots of other little deep
Hub-faced nuns in the wings –
And I took Joachim's hand and hid it
Deep down in my tummy
And he took my hand
And hid it deep down in his shoulder-blades.
Dear woman, I will husband you.
Dear man, I will wife you,
You dandelion you,
You satanic dandy you.
I will wife you
Every day of my life
Pushing up dandelions at the Golden Gate.

SAINTS PETER AND DOROTHY

I am going to marry him, bunions and all,
And I will be the dominant partner.
A nice man is a weak man
And I will be the dominant partner.

Peter?
Dorothy?
Key?
Rosebud?

I am thirty years younger than he
But I like the look of his bunch of keys.
What might I not be able to do
With his bunch of keys.

He is a stoat in spectacles.
Forever taking on and off his spectacles.
Forever hitching up his cloak.
Forever standing in corners protecting his principles.

Perched on the kerb.
You'd think he'd weed his own road.
Dear man, let me be the one to push you over the cliff.
Behind us there is a big blue world out there waiting to drown us.

I am going to marry him, bunions and all,
And I will be the dominant partner.
A nice man is a weak man
And I will be the dominant partner.

The Adoration of the Kings
Jan Gossaert, sometimes called Mabuse

THE ADORATION OF THE KINGS

Jesus Christ is my name.
I was born in Belfast city
But I live in New Zealand,
In the city of Invercargill,
In Southland,
South of Dunedin,
Five miles from Bluff,
Last stop
Before the South Pole.

Back in Belfast
I was known in my time.
Won trophies for table tennis.
My father Joe was a fitter
In the Harland and Wolff shipyard,
A meek, hysterical man
Who always wore red,
Who always saw red;
My mother Mary was a charlady
Who always wore blue,
Always saw blue.

We lived in the gate lodge – one room –
'The Pits' it was called –
Of the ruins of a medieval fortress
In Friendly Street
On the banks of the River Lagan
Right in the city centre,
Five minutes' walk from City Hall.

Every Christmas the politicians used converge on us –
'Everything that crawls must converge.'
They'd haul Mother out into the middle of the ruins
And plonking her down there with her latest pot-bellied babe
(There were seventeen of us)
They'd stage this elaborate, operatic photo call
With them all presenting her with gifts,
'Pressies' they'd croon,
Employing the folksy idiom.
Belfast was a dandy place for the folksy idiom.
They'd arrive dressed up in their folksiest clobber:
All turned out in the latest golfing gear.

And when it wasn't politicians
It was paramilitaries
And when it wasn't paramilitaries
It was press.
Press – I think they were the worst
For palaver. Convoluted bullshit.

Father and Mother were so compliant,
Civil, co-operative with these gaudy chancers,
Especially Mother and yet
Mother was imperturbable.
If your intentions were truly evil
You could not get to her or at her.

Mother was comprehensively insignificant
In the scheme of things in Belfast city.
She had no position on or in anything
Nor did she read newspapers
Except the odd tabloid or watch TV
Except for *Coronation Street*
Or go to poetry readings
Except when her friend Edna'd tell her
They were having Charles Bukowski up at Queens
She'd chuckle: a grand wee man, that Bukowski.
He's like my poor wee Joe, that Bukowski.
In the depths of winter and squalor,
Orgy, murder, universal pretentiousness,
Mother was radiance – a candle in water.
She was placid with a global temper.

These guys – the politicians, the paramilitaries, the press –
They'd go on and on and on and on and on at her
With words. That's what I detested
About them so much – the words – always
The words. Worse than guns words are.
But she'd never react, never.
She'd sit there in contemplation of her body.

Father was a horrible worrier – an armpit of *Angst*.
He'd cast up his eyes to the cameraman, screeching:
'If all these people turned up on your doorstep
When your wife was having a baby, how would you feel?
I need to be taken care of, put away for some time.'
Father knew that to them she was dirt
And that in fact she was dirt
And that she was the mother of God.
That was my father's attitude to women –
He was the sort of man to whom a woman
By definition is the mother of God.

Every Christmas would be the same old pantomime:
The Three Ugly Brothers, each with his hangers-on,
His back slappers, his blurb writers.
One would get down on his knees
Proffering his hands in prayer at Mother's knee
Giving her newborn babe – all navel and curl –
A chalice of coins to commune with.
He'd have a large invisible placard round his neck:
I am a politician, a paramilitary, a pressman
But I am also a man of prayer.

On Mother's right-hand side
There'd be this bonzo in orange suede boots
Who'd have just clapped on a tiara
So in love with himself
That although he'd be holding a gift
It would be to himself he'd be giving it.
He'd spout – never once looking at Mother.
He'd spout poetry – poetry backwards.
He'd awarded himself prizes for his Backwards Poetry

Numero 3 was always the silent type,
The man of few words, the laconic bod
Wanting to get it over with,
Thinking ahead to the next appointment,
The ex-commis waiter balancing his gift in one hand,
Fancying his dexterity. He wrote poetry sideways.

Mind, we never minded the neighbours having a good gawk.
One who always stood opposite Father
Had the most beautiful face in Belfast city.
Nor the boys at the back of the church
Nor the dog rooting about in the broken tiles
Nor the other bitch having a piddle.
Nor Father's donkey. He always kept an ass –
An ass was his grip on reality.

Up in the sky the ubiquitous helicopters,
Crews dangling from them – women with wings
Chatting away on their walkie-talkies for all to hear:
'Do you think baby ought to go to bed?'
'Do you think we should put a stop to it?'
Father would be groaning away
'Don't cry for me, Enniskillen.'
And he'd say to me:
'Christ, get the hell out of here,
It's a slaughterhouse.
All these politicians, paramilitaries, press.
Butchers the lot of them.'

Like most sons
I did not take my father's advice
Until aged thirty-three
I was executed in a football stadium in the suburbs –
Ravenhill Park.

So now I live in New Zealand.
No matter
What my past life may hold
I will never
Go back to Belfast.
Speaking for myself
As Christ the son of Joe and Mary
Let the Kings adore themselves.
Count me out.

Not only do I never want to see
A White Christmas again,
I never want to see any Christmas again.
My own wife here – Mary also –
Maori girl – we live on the *marae* in Island Bay –
She confides in me:
Christ – Christmas is not for you,
Does not agree with you.
She's right.
Christmas is for politicians, paramilitaries, press.
A fairytale to keep butchers happy,
A fairytale to keep the blood flowing –
And the cabbage, the smackers, the tin, the spondulicks, the tickle-tickle.

Jesus Christ is my name:
For me Christianity is not on.

1st February 1993

Portrait of a Young Man
Andrea del Sarto

PORTRAIT OF A YOUNG MAN

If we all of us had a choice of our own death
– And I see no reason why we should not –
I would choose to be murdered by a woman.

I am a man for all mothers.
A woman with whom I'd have slept
Billions of times.

Not with a boning knife. I do not
Like knives, cannot bear the sight of knives.
No. I would like her to smother me with a pillow

Without warning in the middle of a love bout
At the top of her bed, at the height of her passion
To bring the pillow down on my face and I drown

In its ice-blue linen but not before
I put up a stiff resistance, making her
Cry out my name above the traffic and the owls.

It will be twilight in early June mist.
Life is a process of illuminating
A moment to accommodate the inspiration.

Cupid Complaining to Venus
Lucas Cranach the Elder

CUPID COMPLAINING TO VENUS

Like most men
I am a real old genuine
Middle-class puritan.
My wife Juxta –
An abbreviated endearment
For Juxtaposition –
Gambols about our estate naked
And never feels shame.
I envy her.
A life without shame.

I am professor of psychiatry at Jesus
And a TV personality. Professor Cupid.
Always and forever complaining about the state of society.
All my bees in my bonnet.
She is professor of statistics at All Souls.
Uses her maiden name, Venus.
Being a new age man I have taken her name
So that at home we are plain
Madame and Madame Venus.

I adore her.
I adore her filthy toenails.
I adore her thinking woman's mouth.
I adore her small sensible breasts,
Her nipple dexter, her nipple sinister.
I adore her state-of-the-art buttocks.
I adore her whole mucky angle on life.
Her motto: muck in or muck off.
Not like that coy chauvinist Eve's
Slinky cat-in-the-manger angle on life.

I suppose that you could call Juxta
A real Rad Fem don.
Her best friend is a French feminist –
Simone – Simone somebody.
Goes about college starkers.
Her only concession to civilization
(Civilization!)
Is to sport an eighteen-foot necklace and
A hat –
A coconut marshmallow meringue broad-brimmed yokibus.

By day we lead reflective lives,
All water and window,
Urban, suburban, portalled, crenellated.
By night in the privacy of our bedroom
We lead a more active life
In the modern style,
Going out into the forests of our inner selves,
Reversing the roles,
I being the wild doe to her docile stag.
Brandishing her antlers, she crosses her legs
And I nibble her feet.

When Juxta dies
As even Madame Venus must die
And decomposes,
Reverts to forest,
Leaf mould,
I will cherish the memory of her
Swinging out of the trees in Trafalgar Square.
Willie, what would Tarzan say
If his Juxtaposition walked this way?
Juxta Girl Like You.

PORTRAIT OF A MAN
with
SUSANNA LUNDEN

I am a senior warder in the National Gallery.
I detest landscape. They call me Parmigianino
Because I have a habit of glaring at people,
Of looking livid, of wearing my hat in the gallery.
Part of the beauty of the National Gallery
Is that it is tolerant of idiosyncrasy,
Character, old age, youth, beauty, sex.
I like to stand in front of a picture
Looking sideways at it.
I live in – in the National Gallery.
I have a house of my own in Cockfosters
At the end of the Piccadilly Line
But I prefer living in – in the National Gallery
Especially at night when I have it all to myself
And I can walk the galleries alone,
All those nocturnal side issues.

Portrait of a Man
Parmigianino

I have fallen in love once in my life
With a woman. 1954 –
The year Roger Bannister broke the four-minute mile
With the assistance of Chataway –
I fell in love with Susanna Lunden
In Room 22.
Every night for a whole year 1954–55
I sat in front of Susanna Lunden
With a smirk on my face.
In the end I asked her to marry me.
To my surprise, she agreed.
We've been married ever since
Going on forty years
With only the one nark
Which is that she insists on calling me Chataway.
I hiss: Not Chataway. Parmigianino.
Of course, we lead separate lives.
She in her frame in Room 22,
I in my office behind the scenes.
But it works.
There are times in winter in the café
When I am sitting alone in the smoker
That I'd wish for her to be able to join me
And to take off that outrageous felt hat of hers
And to let her red hair down and to listen
To the cheers of the other 250 warders.

Saints Peter and Dorothy
The Master of the Saint Bartholomew Altarpiece

Portrait of Susanna Lunden(?) (Le Chapeau de Paille)
Peter Paul Rubens

She ticks me off: 'My hat synthesises
For me my freedom. Besides
I enjoy having my portrait painted.
The painter Peter Paul Rubens
Puts me up on a pedestal in his little black room
And for hours he crawls about on the floor.
Staring up at me and saying things like
"Don't look at my face, dearie, look at my bum",
Or "Don't hand me the hatchet, dearie, just throw it."
People often ask me what I'm thinking.
I am thinking what a nice man Peter Paul Rubens is
And how I'd like to parcel him up and take him away with me
And play with him for two weeks – just two weeks –
Not more than two weeks. I am sure
He would be great fun to play with for two weeks
And then he'd go off and continue his great career
And I would always think of him with affection
And never meet him again.
That's what my portrait means to me – affection.
It is painted with affection by a man –
The sort of man who even with his pants down
Would rather make the effort
To let a fly live than to swat it.
Affection – I cannot have enough of it – affection.'

But such is life – even in Trafalgar Square.
At least we have every night together.
I sit alone in front of her in the dark
– Nocturnal Seed –
And when my hip flask is empty
She replenishes it from her bosom
– She always carries cash in her bosom –
– A bit of a solicitor in respect of cash –
And as I take a fresh swig
She smiles that convent girl smile of hers
That says: Mmm, Nocturnal Seed, Mmm.

A LADY WITH A SQUIRREL AND A STARLING

Mother has a habit of scratching her groin
But that does not irritate me half as much
As when after having dolloped herself with face cream
She stands in her window at night
Staring out into the fig trees
Stacked with larks,
Her squirrel in her hands,
Its tail between her breasts.

It's the tail
In Mother's bosom
That causes me pain,
That causes me panic.
I want to put out my hand
And snuff it – the tail –
Or to thwack it.
Then Mother's breastline
Would be as it ought to be,
All of a piece,
Symmetrical, immaculate, jointed
In its underdress of fine linen of cambric.

But I never do
Put out my hand
And the sun sets on my anger.

A LADY WITH A SQUIRREL AND A STARLING
Hans Holbein the Younger

'Son, let the sun never
Set on your anger.'
Will I ever learn
To accept Mother as she is?

Young girl at heart that she is,
Garrulous hermit,
Trueblue trueturquoise loncr,
A lady with a squirrel and a starling.

She never complains about *me*.
Never remarks upon my foible,
A gentleman with a moose and a vagary.

Ignore him, Mum,
Ad infinitum, ignore him, ignore him.

The Death of Actaeon
Titian

THE DEATH OF ACTAEON

I am slumped on my horse
In the woods of my own self
Watching Actaeon die
In Ladbroke Grove;
Actaeon, my closest friend,
England's finest painter.
His wife Diana, tall, fair,
With her bow but no bowstring,
Is striding in for the kill.
Her torrent of anger at her side.
Her skies of resentment at her back,
Her ground of bitterness at her feet.

Actaeon had his heart
Set on Diana from the start.
When he chanced to meet her
Bathing naked in the river,
Naked at its source,
She demanded from him intercourse.
Such was her delight
She invited him that same night
To make a home with her
And her four Alsatians.
Overnight he became
The most celebrated painter in London town,
Exhibiting annually in New York and Berlin.
Actaeon could do no wrong
Because Diana was his song.

After ten years of matrimony
On her thirtieth birthday
She threw him out of the matrimonial home:
Enough of being your song.
Actaeon went to live in a bar
On the corner of Ladbroke Grove
And Westbourne Park Road.
He never painted again.
He grew minusculer and minusculer,
He lost weight and height,
Until he became by day
A stag at bay,
A glass of whisky in his cloven hand,
A haunted sizzle in his eyes.
Even the four dogs felt pity for him
Caressing him in his throes.

It is chamber music to his young wife
To watch Actaeon die.
She feels reborn in the light of his dying.
His dying casts a new light over everything,
Has given her something to live for.
A flaming feminist
She strides down Ladbroke Grove
Past clumps of narcissi.
Gutters in spate.
Amber lamplight of streetlamps
Lighting up her crimson négligé.
She strides out with her right breast exposed,
Her nipple erect.
She strides out Ladbroke Grove
To the Television Centre in Shepherd's Bush
To present her own arts show on TV –
A documentary on the life and work
Of the greatest English painter of our time,
The Actaeon Trilogy.

At the moment of transmission
Actaeon is standing at the bar
Being held up by hangers on
As he swallows his own tongue.
There is nothing anyone can do for Actaeon
Because Actaeon adores the woman
Who is killing him. Actaeon
Will not hear a word against his goddess;
He adores his woman because she is killing him.
He croaks: Give me your hand.
The film expires in scarlet and gold
With Actaeon crawling on his hands and knees
Slurping brandy from her hand.
The art world's comet
Chokes in his own vomit.

THE SUPPER AT EMMAUS

The light of evening, Emmaus,
Small windows open to the south,
Two old brothers, both
Beautiful, dying of Alzheimer's disease.
Do you remember the Englishman?
No, I do not remember the Englishman.

The Supper at Emmaus
Michelangelo Merisi da Caravaggio

In the pub at Emmaus
My brother and I
Chance to glance up
And who do we see
Seated at our table
But a familiar stranger,
Salman Rushdie
– Red smock, white sari –
Breaking bread with God.

As if breaking bread with God
Is the most normal, natural,
Sacred, profane
Thing in the world to do.
God says to the pair of us:
I am Salman Rushdie.
Outside in the back lanes of Emmaus
A mob clubs to death a lone man.

We catch a glimpse of God;
His conscience;
His bread, His fruit, His wine;
His search for justice through creativity.

The publican Gabriel – a responsible publican –
Is standing behind God.
Giving God a message.
Obviously Gabe – as he is known in Emmaus –
Gabe's Place is the name of the pub –
'Gabe's For The Crack' as the logo has it –
Obviously Gabe has had a phonecall
From a certain party.

'Tell God –
We are coming to get Him.
He must say goodbye
To Dermot and Colm.'

My brother's sari slips down round his thighs.
I sit up with my arms held out,
All my years as a goalkeeper behind me,
Knowing that this is the penalty kick
And that I am going to save it
And that at the end of time –
At the end of extra time –
Nobody will remember it.
Or they will say: who?
Or: where?

Do you remember the Englishman?
No, I do not remember the Englishman.

Christ Appearing to Saint Peter on the Appian Way
(Domine Quo Vadis?)
Annibale Carracci

CHRIST AND SAINT PETER ON THE APPIAN WAY

Not drowning but waving.

Buoyant on the Appian Way
Outside Niall and Hop Montgomery's house
At a junction of roads of equal importance

Uncle Peter is waiting to tell me
That I will fail my driving test
Or that, if I pass it, I will die on the road.

My death is the lightest cross I have to bear.
I can toss it from here to there.
Dying is hopping a stone off water.

It is my soul that poses the question.
It is my soul that is the weight of the world.
It is my soul that is in search of observation and progress.

Only reality can save me.
Human kind can bear
An awful lot of reality.

I propose that for the first time in history
You also go it alone – that you no longer shrink
From going out there and doing your driving test.

Not drowning but waving.

Samson and Delilah
Peter Paul Rubens

SAMSON AND DELILAH II

I am a master barber
Trained in Cleveland, Ohio
Working in Antwerp, Belgium
For the Maison Philistine
Chain of Hairdressing Salons.
I employ the left-hand-over-
The-right-hand technique.
I am absorbed in the job
But I am aware of the silence
And of the knives in the doorway.
She whispers to me: He make the big love.
I whisper: He what?
She whispers: He make the big love.
I concur: He make the big love.
She whispers: He like Tom Jones.
I concur: He like Tom Jones.
She whispers: He do the whole intercourse –
Not just middle
But beginning end middle.
He jump up, he jump down.
He carry me around room.
He put me down.
He caress me.
He lie under me.
He lie over me.
He drink me.
He eat me.
He wait for me until I am so far out
I think I am going to vanish my throat.

– Delilah, I am dreaming.
– My little puss dreaming?
– Dreaming I am having a haircut.
– Silly Samson.
– Are you cross with me, Delilah?
– Course not, little puss, course not.
– Am I going to die, Delilah?
– A little dying, silly Samson, a little dying.

PORTRAIT OF GOVAERT VAN SURPELE AND HIS WIFE

My husband is a vain man
But he is not conceited.
As Freddy Ayer used say:
'I like the medals I own
But I do not begrudge
The other fellow *his* medals.'

My husband is a problem.
Every husband is a problem.
He is an E.E.C. Commissioner
Who fancies himself as a poet,
A diplomatic troubadour,
And I am his muse to amuse

Our dinner-party guests.
When dinner is done and just
As we are all in danger of relaxing
He pops up at the head of the table,
Bangs his staff on the floor, calls me
'My spring lamb, my perennial parrot.'

I smile. I smile a ghostly smile.
When the guests depart it will be my turn.
Mountainous we are – the pair of us.
Not ruinous – mountainous.
The Alps – we're known as in Brussels' social circles.
I'm his Mont Blanc. He's my Matterhorn.

Portrait of Govaert van Surpele(?) and His Wife
Jacob Jordaens

As Mr and Mrs Alp we lead an intense private life.
We like ruling you all from Brussels.
At our altitude it gets really hot in our home.
Life with central heating
Turned up full all the time.
Only aircraft get in our way.

But he does tend to go on with his poems,
To inflict his poems on visitors.
Epics celebrating the Brussels male's capacity
To urinate in grand public places.
The way he struts there spouting with his left hand
Flung down backwards on his poncy thigh.

When the guests depart and after
I've hung him up by the heels and embraced him
I take him down and throw him into bed.
I bleat: Footstool, your motto.
How he loves to bark: Have Paunch, Will Stay
Put where I am, never travel, rule my patch
  with a rod of iron and by all men be feared
    and by thee be adored, so there, wifey, so there, wallop.

THE GROTE KERK, HAARLEM

I

I am not one of the bitter brethren.
Churches are a part of my life
As essential as cinemas or cafés.

THE GROTE KERK, HAARLEM
Pieter Saenredam

In the autumn of Central Europe
The thrill of city life is, being borne along
In the crowd in a centre city street,
Suddenly to slip without warning to oneself
Into one of the hundreds of churches;
In less than four or five seconds to slip out of tumult
Into stillness – out of attitude into repose –
Out of the journalism of adulthood
Into the science fiction of childhood.

The day Daddy took me to church
As I watched him kneeling in his pew
I stood up on my hind legs and wagged my tail.
As I gazed up into Daddy's praying face
Under his great broad-brimmed black hat
It was I who was an appendage to my tail.
My tail stiffened in an arc of pure affection
And yelping I went bounding off into Mother's vaults
Returning to him in a lump at his feet.

II

In the Grote Kerk in Haarlem
I kneel with my hat on and rejoice
That in the year 1637 it is also 2001;
Rejoice also in the emptiness of my soul.
My son extends himself and my daughter squats
On the floor shelling peas.

III

Shelling peas in church
I passed from girlhood into womanhood
And became a doctor.

IV

I go back out into the street
Ramified that I am a spaceman;
That my soul is a spaceship;
That my soul is a nosedrip chandelier
Drooping down by golden threads to the floor;
That my father is roundy but my mother is pointy;
That my soul is supra modern, supra medieval,
Black on white;
That my soul is at its core a Russian icon;
That if my now-name is Andrei Tarkovsky
My always-name is Andrei Rublyev;
That my soul is a hospital on a city street
In Haarlem painting the night-time white:
That my soul is my doctor daughter.

Step –
Step into me.

Cardinal Richelieu
Philippe de Champaigne

CARDINAL RICHELIEU

Mother, I do appreciate how chuffed
You must be that your son is a cardinal
But it is a hard old station staying off the drink.

You in your turn must appreciate
That what takes precedence in my life
Is not you or wine but my red biretta.

Life now is all a matter of biretta.
I have got to think biretta, sleep biretta, eat biretta.
No more booze. Biretta biretta.

Life is a cruel rota of checks and balances.
Of suppressing the shakes. Of mints and lozenges.
Of learning to hold on to one's biretta.

I take lessons every morning.
Eighteen holes before breakfast.
Drinking golfers call me 'The Dry Biretta'.

Mother, you above all should understand
If I so much as once drop my biretta
All my knickers will seize up,

My palaces of knickers,
My lace girdles, my frilly panties,
My starched collars, all my taffeta.

Mother, you above all know without censure
What a ponce I am – the way I comb
My hair back over my skull cap

In a quiff – quite against the rules –
And my sneer. A seventeenth-century teddy boy.
All that concupiscence tethered to etiquette.

For you alone, Mother, I unhitch my capa magna,
Don my biretta, dance you out on to the patio poolside.
Draw a gold curtain over our relationship.

I'm all right, Ma, I'm only manic.

A FAMILY GROUP IN A LANDSCAPE

Being the eldest of seven and the first daughter
I am always hanging out on the edge
With my handbag – all my bits and bobs –
Composed in my reticent way
Watching the little ones at play
At Mama's and Papa's knees.

A Family Group in a Landscape
Frans Hals

The gosling all in white
In the crook of the arm of our Nurse
Is about to be foisted with a rose
By her brother; Papa's and Mama's eyes
On the apple in my hand; at the last minute
He withholds the rose. Boys oh boys.

He drops to his knee and he
Holds up the rose before her eyes
And he begins to gasp like a gander
Whispering 'Give me your hand'
And he careers off into the green and gold sky
Stocked with bullocks and gloom.

Happy Families is our favourite game
In spite of the bullocks and gloom.
No matter how grim things are –
Our black-and-white buttoned up attire –
We never have to pose for the family photograph.
In our formal menagerie we are informal.

Mainly thanks to our mother and father.
Mama was one of eight, Papa one of eleven.
They are all hands, the pair of them,
Which is why I suppose we are all hands.
Nine pairs of hands, not counting Nurse's.
Girls and their baskets, boys oh boys.

Beyond Haarlem, out on the edge of the coast,
An old woman in bed with a jug of gin
Blaze upon blaze of coastal attrition.
Her ear to the sea under her bedroom window.

'Family Life O Family Life;
In need of a landscape we were loaned a landscape
Until the lender burnt our landscape down.
The Family that dies together lives together.'

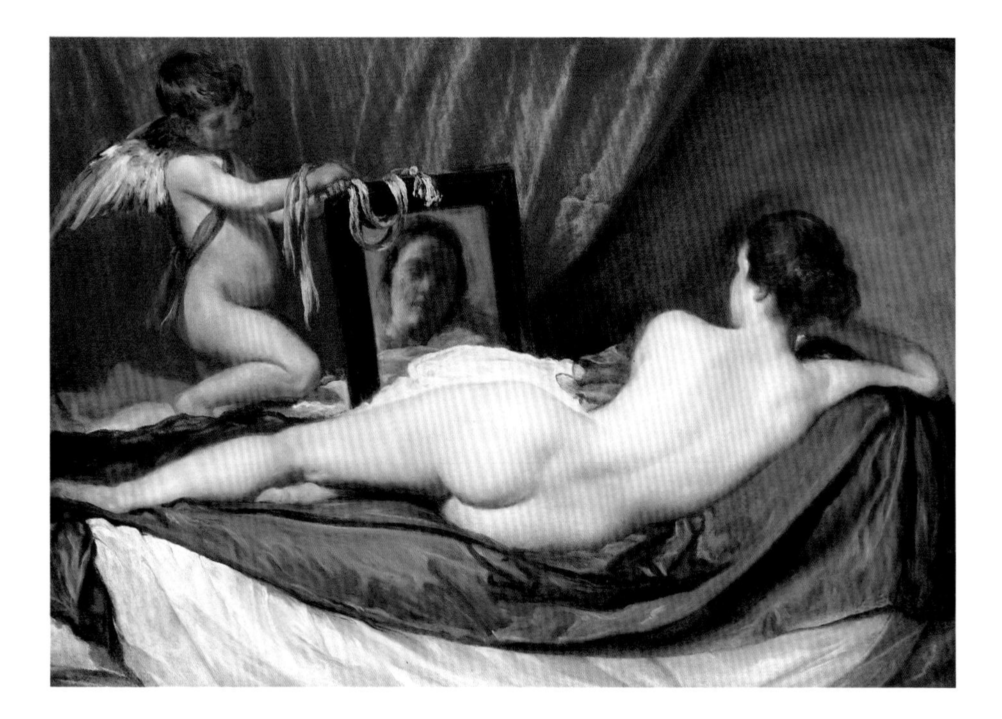

The Toilet of Venus (The Rokeby Venus)
Diego Velázquez

THE ROKEBY VENUS

I lie on my bed
In the raw watching videos.

Soap after soap,
Weeping my eyes out.

On a Yorkshire moor
A kicked-over heap of tears.

Is that not what a woman is –
A kicked-over heap of tears?

Pity.
Pity about men.

THE ANNUNCIATION
Nicolas Poussin

THE ANNUNCIATION

Compose me.

Not all viola players are mothers
But all mothers are viola players.

Tune me.

Your mild, mild daughter.
Your wild, wild virgin.

Rehearse me.

My toes, my knees, palms of my hands,
My throat, my breast, strings of my stomach.

Conduct me.

In the tail of my plane
Come, come to me.

I am dead happy.

Flying home to Bethlehem
To give birth to the Music Man.

Dead, dead, dead happy.

A Sleeping Maid and Her Mistress
Nicolaes Maes

INTERIOR WITH A SLEEPING MAID AND HER MISTRESS

Maids are gone to pot.
Look at my maid.
Look at her. The puss on her.
Depression, no less.
What next?
Complains that she is worn out
From having to make love to my son.
What does she think I pay her for?
For washing up dishes?
For scouring pans?
For walloping pots?
My dear little son Tom
Likes his slice of breast
And he is a curious little boy
Which is why I pay her a penny a week
To instruct him in the facts of life
And to keep it clean in my kitchen.
A penny a week may not be much to you
But it is a lot to me
Married as I am to a stockbroker in Godalming.
I have my hands full
– The Lord love me –
Playing daylight Bridge
In the front parlour.

River Landscape with Horseman and Peasants
Aelbert Cuyp

RIVER LANDSCAPE WITH HORSEMAN AND PEASANTS

Such so is the silence of evening,
Only the din of traffic hum,
That neither of us passes any comment
Watching the marksman down on his knees
Taking aim at the pair of us across the pond
Of the Broad Walk,
A pair of duck.

A single shot rings out.
I think I am dead.
Stephen thinks he is dead.
Then I think Stephen is dead.
Then he thinks I am dead.
We are alive. He has missed.
We begin sobbing, putting our arms around one another,
Tentacles of tenderness, silence resuming its sniping
Over London, Belfast, Sarajevo.

The Rest on the Flight into Egypt
Adriaen van der Werff

THE REST ON THE FLIGHT INTO EGYPT

I

My only son
Died aged thirty-three of Aids.
I nursed him in Egypt
At the end.
Sat by him
Day and night for six months.
He grew so small.
Dwindled down.
A little stick
Of birthday candle,
All grease and wick.
O my Tartar
Petal.

II

O my little man
There is light on the oak leaves.
Try not to dwell
On what's ahead of us,
Your father asleep on the road behind us,
Your father asleep on the road before us.
Let me play the lute of your soul,
Your small male skull.
With my maternal fingers
Let me work the strings
Of your right leg,
Hear out your penis's
  Bitter sweet hiss.

Let me apply my lipstick to you,
My nipple, my lip.
Let us not fret
On this night of nights,
Light of lights,
After four hundred million years of being together.
He goes out as he came in –
On a woman's arm, alone.
O my Tartar
Petal.

MR AND MRS ANDREWS

Tweet-tweet-tweet-tweet-tweet-tweet-tweet.
Twitter-twitter-twitter-twitter-twitter-twitter-twitter.
Boo-boo-boo-boo-boo-boo-boo
He is sulking because he wants his din-dins.

MR AND MRS ANDREWS
Thomas Gainsborough

Fanning myself in the Suffolk desert
I mince round a corner of horizon
And there midst all that silly sand
Is a wrought-iron garden seat
Peeking out of old oak tree,
Stooks, sheepies, poppy
And, choreographed on seat,
Oneself.

The sort of dream out of which stuff is made.
Oneself
In most à la modish blue frock,
Pink high heel slippers,
Floppy hat,
And, lounging up against rail of seat
Like a skimpy stag against its scratching post,
One's very own chap,
A spaniel in his parts
Sniffing,
Taking time off from his economics lectures
Or his ballet classes or whatever.

Bobsie Andrews and Me:
We two drips together dripping.
I murder him
With his own gun.
The nice thing is that the neighbours
Think it an accident.

I think my feeling was that I did not really want
To have to share the landscape.
It is a rather fetching landscape
In spite of all the suffocation
And I think I will rather enjoy it on my own
For the next fifty years
And not spoil it with children and inheritance
And all that sort of thing.
Fetch.

Exhibition of a Rhinoceros at Venice
Pietro Longhi

EXHIBITION OF A RHINOCEROS IN VENICE

I remember winter afternoons in strip clubs in Soho
In the company of witty lawyers
And thinking that I had known much more engrossing times
And that was when I was a teenage girl in Venice
And Mother used drag me along to the women's club –
The Jane Austen Reading Club in a disused church
Where they kept a rhinoceros on exhibition in the sanctuary.
Mother and her accomplices used saunter about the pews
In masks, tricorn hats, fans.
At first I thought the fans were for dispelling smells
But later I realized they were for something else,
Something to do with sudden heat.

Nowadays whenever I find myself alone in a lift
With a rhinoceros
I have no need of fans, masks, hats.
To be a woman alone with a rhinoceros in a lift
Is to feel quite – quite ludicrous.
I enjoy it enormously.

I enjoy it enormously.
Too often nowadays in these rancorous
Politically correct times
I find myself alone in a lift
Without a rhinoceros.

The Painter's Daughters Chasing a Butterfly
Thomas Gainsborough

THE PAINTER'S DAUGHTERS CHASING A BUTTERFLY

Little sister and I – there is a year between us –
Although we are different as chalk and cheese
We are the closest of friends and my deepest fear
Is of something happening to her. I have dreams
Of her being shredded in car crashes on black ice
Or of her mistaking cockroach powder for Parmesan cheese.

In the dream of life she and I
Are a pair of butterflies.
I am holding her hand as in her wilfulness
– She makes Eve Defying look like Eve Demurring –
She chases every single butterfly she ever sees.

Although we both detest Fisticuffs
(Dad loves it!)
Our favourite motto is Muhammad Ali's
'Float like a butterfly, sting like a bee,
Rumble, man, rumble.'
Little sister and I
Love to rumble in the woods,
Meet small, dark, bright-voiced, uncouth boys,
Thistles under butterflies.

Our mother and father are also butterflies
Separated but inseparable.
Thistles incompatible.
We are closest to Mum but Dad is daft about us
And we are fond of him provided
That he does not overdo the torch.
That is Dad's problem – the torch.
This Yuletide – Noël! Noël! –
We received a letter from him in Sudbury
(We dwell in London with Mum)
Specifying what he wants from Santa Claus:

A head-torch!
He writes: I am getting on in years
And when I lose my way in the woods at night
On my way home from Gentle Annie's
I would like to be able to consult my bible –
That is to say, my ordnance survey map, my dears –
By the light of a decent flame in my forehead
Like any other sinner on this god-forsaken, blasted earth.

He says we can purchase the head-torch in any odd shop in London.
We reckon that he owns at least five thousand torches,
The majority of them hand-torches,
But also backside-torches, navel-torches, groin-torches.
I am an artist – is his great excuse –
I am not afraid to live by the light of my own darkness.
The only time he ever comes to London
Is when there is a Lucien Freud exhibition.

Fathers like to beam torches in their daughters' faces,
Especially in their eldest daughters' faces.

Darlingest Dad, – We will be down on Boxing Day
Or at least at the very latest
By the Feast of the Epiphany
Provided you promise not to overdo it with the head-torch.
We will chase lots and lots and lots of butterfly
With you, you silly old butterfly you.
Meg is going to bring her new white dress
And I will be in gold – as usual. Pigs of love. Mary.

Mr and Mrs Thomas Coltman
Joseph Wright of Derby

MR AND MRS THOMAS COLTMAN

If I wasn't a filly –
A wise, feminine creature,
I'd trample you to death, sir,
You concupiscent doggy you.

Good riddance
To the days when we had five hundred servants.
Mr Coltman and I
Manage – make do – with a skeleton staff
Of between ten and twenty:
Ten in winter, twenty in summer.
We've opened Red Gables to the public
As a country house hotel:
We are members of 'The Real England'
Group of country-house hotels,
Discreet, homely, expensive B & B's.

I say 'Mr' Coltman
But actually we're not married
In the eighteenth-century sense.
We're partners
In the twentieth-century sense.
I discovered him one night
In the Irish Embassy
When I was doing meals-on-wheels,
Brought him home,
Bathed him in the trough,
Fitted him up in my
Ex's Marks and Sparks pin-stripe pyjamas.
(My ex has gone into the bathroom tile business
With our stable girl.)
He's a damn decent sort – my new Tom –
And as well as working his butt off
He gives me a lot of love and affection
Which I appreciate.
Like any other man he can be
Demonstrably oafish
(Cuddling me when I'm in the middle
Of cooking quails' eggs
For the visitors' children's breakfast)
But it's more than worth it
For his utopian proclivities.

Then there is always Sunday
Morning to look forward to
When I go for a ride on Wallace,
My old grey mare,
And Tom walks us out to the beech tree
And gives me his weekly
Sermon on the mount
On the history of the Tory Party
About which I knew absolutely nothing.
Until I met Tom
I used to think Edward Heath
Was a colony in East Africa
And that Tha'Tcher was a French technique in Foreplay.

On a Sunday morning under a cold blue sky
I love to sit sidesaddle on my grey
In my brick-red riding skirts
And my braided blouse
And my hat with swans' feathers
And Tom behaving himself beneath me
Within the orb of my riding crop
Resting his elbow in my lap.
I am the queen of all I survey;
The conscience of the wealth of nations;
Sovereign of pebbles, beachboys, dirt, leaves.

I find it so life-enhancing
While he's mumbling on about the old church tower
And how every human being has a certain power.
Of course we don't go to church anymore
(This *is* the last decade of the twentieth century)
But gazing down upon Tom's dear little head
(He has a much bigger head than most men I know)
I can perceive a spiritual dimension.
I savour the bite of his companionship,
The biscuit of mortality.
Life with my infant man
Is one long perpetual Boxing Day.
Dear visitor, when you can
Do come to Red Gables,
Do be our guest:
We are the Real England.
(However, it would be appreciated if on arrival
Guests would go straight to bed.)

If I wasn't a filly –
A wise, feminine creature,
I'd trample you to death, sir,
You concupiscent doggy you.

MADAME DE POMPADOUR

Here's what it all comes down to – the big L.
I am so lonely I could murder you –
You upon whom I have never set eyes
Until this instant in Room 33
You Spartan you.

Do you like my dress?
Clever, isn't it?
Chamber-pots on hooks?
I am waiting for his nibs.
Any year now
He will come charging
Down the spiral staircase,
Fling open the door,
Strip off his panties,
Kick aside my tapestry frame,
Undo my lace cap,
Cast my flowered dress all over my worktable,
Spill all my bales of wool,
Not to mention my chamber-pots,
Dip his finger in my navel and bless himself
Roaring 'I am the King.'
The terrible thing is
That I will love every minute of it.

Madame de Pompadour
François-Hubert Drouais

He will moan 'I miss you, I miss you',
But he will not mean a word of it.
Or will he?
And then –
And then quick as you'd snap
A mandolin gut
It's over
And he is back into being his barking old self again,
Being a wee black dog,
Bébé, Bébé,
And he races back upstairs
To his kennel in the skies of Versailles.

My double chin
That seconds ago was just one chinkin
Re-instates itself
And hangs about my bare walls
Waiting to be tweaked
And I resume my existence here sitting alone
Being a patron of the arts
Or – when you out there are not staring at me –
Beating bean bags.

I like the way I hang
Facing Sparta.
Of all the bodies of the *ancien régime*
The body of Madame de Pompadour
Hangs just so, don't you agree?
I think it would be best if you agree.

General Sir Banastre Tarleton
Joshua Reynolds

GENERAL SIR BANASTRE TARLETON

I wanted my son to play for England,
To play at out-half for England,
And he did – against France in Twickenham.
On a typical Saturday afternoon in February,
Dull, overcast,
All of fifty years ago.
He rode up for the game that day
On a red Hunter, black plumed hat,
Skintight breeches, hunting jacket,
He was that on fire about it all.

In my wheelchair on the seafront at Brighton
Gazing out across the sea to France
I can see him out there in the grey field,
His drowned red hair flowing behind him,
In the very act and combination of kicking
The drop goal from play that won the game
For England and Northampton:
In the very act of preparing to kick
He bends ever so slightly
To pull up his sock and tie up his garter
And he has his two hands on his thighs
And as he steals a quick glance at his scrum half
He inhales, exhales, the smoky February air.
As the ball zips into his hands
(He had a superb pair of hands – the boy,
The safest hands in the UK – they used say)
He does not even trouble to look up at the French posts,
He stares down at the oval ball in his hands
– The prey, the sacred prey –
And drop kicks it into the sky between the posts.

In after years, of course, they tried,
As is the current fashion in Great Britain and Ireland,
To take his name and character from him
When he died last year from Aids.
But his wife stood by him, always did.
Decent girl, always was.
They say he was gay. Oh
He was gay all right, my boy, he was gay all right.
Dear brave sweet tender genial Banastre.

I am bloody awful lonely here in Brighton
On the seafront in my wheelchair
In the front lines of old age,
The great guns booming across the Channel
From France as they have always done
And always will. War is in the nature of life
Like love. The two things go together.
You cannot have love without war *and*
– *And* I say (this is what
Those buggers in the tabloids as well as in the quality
Press, suppress) – you cannot have war without love.

Dear dear Banastre! The old woman
On fire in the wheelchair beside me is a she-bear
And I – as she says – am a little old monkey
With silver hair and my private parts
Are bits of gold – tarnished gold.
I lean over and insert my little finger in her garter.
Bloody awful lonely here in Brighton, son.
Bloody awful lonely here in Paradise, sir.
Goodnight, General.
Goodnight, Father.

Young Ladies on the Bank of the Seine
Jean-Désiré-Gustave Courbet

YOUNG LADIES ON THE BANK OF THE SEINE

In the chicest restaurant on the left bank –
The Artist's Studio –
We have installed a black, gaudy fish tank
Containing women dressed as lobsters.
Male diners may order the women of their choice
Which is not to say hastily that female diners
May not also order the women of their choice,
They may. But not men of their choice.
The Artist's Studio restaurant serves only
And exclusively female lobsters.

This evening we have two female lobsters
Waiting their turn to be boiled alive.
Although they are wearing their best carapaces
One has to acknowledge a certain fatalism in their faces.

The Stove in the Studio
Paul Cézanne

THE STOVE IN THE STUDIO

Father
I attend your stovepipe;
I poke your red coals;
Eat you.

Mother
I attend your pot;
Grip your handles;
Drink you.

Trite to talk
Of four walls;
No walls, only you two –
Black space of the world.

The stove in the studio:
By the light of a stretcher
I will live my death.
P. Cézanne

YOUNG SPARTANS

That summer my parents decided to skip
The caravan in Weston-super-Mare,
Opting instead for a central London hotel,
The Sparta in the Strand
Around the corner from Trafalgar Square.
We spent every day in Trafalgar Square
Moping about with other boys and girls,
Holding hands, not holding hands,
Sulking, preening, teasing, posing,
Trying to think of something to rap about,
Trying out cigarettes, alcohol, dope,
Trying out the latest tie-dyed T-shirts,
Patched stonewashed jeans thinking themselves
Cooler than brand-new cords;
The code, the etiquette, the protocol;
A gaffe here, a gaffe there;
Bits and pieces of merriment in the universal embarrassment.

One day in July a Northern Ireland clergyman
With woolly grey hair, specs, a sexy voice,
The Reverend Humphrey Rooney, arrived into the hotel
'For a wee sabbatical,' he drawled and all our mothers
Got the hots on him, and they followed him around
Hanging on his every word and all our dads
Sat behind their *Daily Telegraph*s and their *Guardian*s
Cowering in wine-red jealousy
Having to listen to the Reverend spouting his Belfast blarney
About 'the Young Folk – the Young Folk of Today'.

Reverend Humphrey Rooney was a big shot in the Queen's University,
A big chief in the ideology of education.
He tongue-lashed our mothers as they knelt at his feet
Worshipping his eyebrows – his wild boar eyebrows –
That their children's problems were problems of garments,
That adolescents needed to be protected from garment manufacturers.
He prowled round our mothers: What adolescents need
Is to be given back into their own original pristine
Nature that the Good Lord has vouchsafed them.

YOUNG SPARTANS EXERCISING
Hilaire-Germain-Edgar Degas

Thank God for that old Belfast panther.
That was the day I became a blonde teenager
Naked on my hands and knees
In Trafalgar Square.
At last I was a teenager,
Pimples and all.
At last childhood was over.
Childhood is a gross state of affairs;
All that innocence and tranquillity
Recollected in emotion.
Jesus, do not put me back
Into the short pants of innocence.

On my hands and knees
I looked up and saw a young woman
Poised opposite me
In black loincloth, red belt.
Sizing me up, taking me in,
Twittering like a starling – a stare –
She was winding up for the high jump,
Winding up to unleash herself.

She landed spot-on in the small of my back.
We were made for each other.
Sixty years on
At dusk if you care to stroll the Strand
Past the Sparta Hotel
Heading towards Trafalgar Square
You can see me taking her out for a walk;
I on my hands and knees as ever,
She elegant as ever, red hair tied up,
Sitting astride my back.
O Man, born for serving Woman.
I have served her well in peace and war,
In bed and on the street,
In the kitchen and in the bathroom,
Served her because I was born to:
Servus servorum Dei.

Terrifying – how could it be other than terrifying?
(At the Last Judgement it is not so much the Judgement
That is terrifying as the faces in the public gallery –
Familiar faces last seen sixty years ago.)
Terrifying what becomes of us all.
All of us boys ill-at-ease in our bodies:
What to do with all these permanent erections?
All of the girls ill-at-ease in their bodies:
What to do with all these blood stains?

My friend Sam – the tallest of us –
Who the instant he'd see a girl prowling
He'd put his hands up in the air,
Join his hands above his head,
Spin himself into a ball –
Sam took Ann in the red headband
To Perth in Western Australia
Despite the efforts of her sister to restrain her.
They divorced in Perth in Western Australia
But at least they went out there,
Followed their own noses, sang their own songlines.

Maurice the Runner – we were all athletes –
All fancied ourselves as four-minute milers –
Was a sucker for bashful taunts
And he ran straight into the arms
Of Stephanie who got her hooks into him,
Reduced him to skin and bone
Before she deposited him in Scunthorpe
In favour of a Scunthorpe man.
Louis Redhead never married,
Stayed a bachelor boy,
Ultra conservative, ultra respectable,
Bumping the kips at night.

Denis the Boxer married Ann's sister
And lived happily ever after
In the grief common to us all.
In time we most of us drowned
And became parents ourselves
Fussing in the middle ground
In thrall to gurus pontificating,
Watching our own daughters and sons
Shaping up for the contest,
For yet another Rumble in the National,
Another Rave in the Square,
Another summer in the Sparta Hotel,
The combat
That women always win:
Give me your hand.

Miss La La at the Cirque Fernando
Hilaire-Germain-Edgar Degas

LA LA AT THE CIRQUE FERNANDO, PARIS

Ever since I hanged myself
In the doorway of my bedroom
Of the house in Yelabuga
On the banks of the Kama
In the limbo summer of 1941
Ground Control keep asking:
What was going on in your mind?
What were you thinking?
Ground Control, please listen.

Everyone had gone out of the house for the day
Fishing – for fish, for anything.
I was sitting there moping,
A bird woman sans hope in middle age,
When I lifted my head
And glimpsing a woodthrush
On the bough at the window
I glimpsed La La at the Cirque Fernando
In Paris when I was a girl
In January 1878.
I had wasted my life as a poet
Out of wanting to emulate La La,
Out of wanting to be
Like La La
A thing with wings.

Papa it was
Who took me to the Cirque
To watch La La.
At first he said she had escaped
– Escaped from what? – a cage? –
And I held his hand tight
With awe and in fright
But then when he saw my tears
He said there'd been a mistake,
That she had not escaped,
And I let go of his hand
And they began to raise up La La
On the pulley rope.

There was a length of rope
On the floor in the corner
And I who could never
Do anything with my hands
Except tie up my shoes,
Threaded the rope through
A nail in the lintel.
I tied it up to the stove.
I climbed up on the straight-backed chair,
The only chair in the room,
And with my hands swinging by my side,
Swimming out the bay,
I who have washed my teeth
Every day of my life
I cried out 'La La'
Kicking the chair away.

There in that black and white hole,
The town of Yelabuga,
On the banks of the Kama,
My white hair turned black,
My black underwear turned white,
And I was a furry, uncut, silky thing
Marching up the sky to Montparnasse
To drink cognac with my men,
And I began to climb
Higher and higher
Into the purple and gold of my girlhood,
All my day things
Far down below me in the sawdust
And the stalls.

Swinging my arms in the orange cumulus,
Putting my knees through the black windows,
Kicking away the green hedgerows,
Crossing my feet in prayer,
My hands becoming me,
I becoming my hands,
Never ever
Having to speak again,
Never ever
Having to crawl on my hands
At the feet of editors,
All the world was taut,
I was speed itself
And O my God it was hot
Up there
Just like it was with you in bed
O my daughter,
When I gave birth to you.

When they cut the rope,
The cord,
I fell in an aftermath on the floor,
A cold cold aftermath
On the cold cold floor.
A lady in the front row
– Was she my mother?
– I think she was my mother –
Asked: What's that?
My father said: La La.

O Watcher of the skies,
O parquet crawler,
Let me go free,
Let me fly back up into my future,
Into my frame,
Don't let me
Continue to lie
Dead at your feet,
Don't let me
Be a poet,
A bird in a snare,
A rat in a trap.

Let me fly back up into the rafters,
Into the girders,
Into the span of life,
The great hall of the earl,
Window to window,
Woodthrush,
Fluff,
La La.

Poetry is a lie.
Only that which is not poetry
Is true.

Drop me.

'The Rosy Wealth of June'
Ignace-Henri-Jean-Théodore Fantin-Latour

'THE ROSY WEALTH OF JUNE'

Do you think I do not notice
Up there amongst the rockets and the begonias,
The delphiniums and the lilies,
All those subtle, aristocratic roses,
Those two dahlias
Brooding to drink my blood?

On a dead Sunday afternoon in June
In a cul-de-sac in Twickenham
In a detached villa in an exclusive suburb
Two dahlias
Without anyone noticing their presence
Brooding to stab me to death?

Two dahlias
Dallying in a mass of roses
– Face powder pink and blush white –
To revenge themselves on my lord?

Ignace-Henri-Jean-Théodore Fantin-Latour
Master flower painter,
All in the rosy wealth of June
I accuse you of the perfect murder –
The softest of rose-pinks darkening towards the centre.

A Cornfield, with cypresses
Vincent van Gogh

A CORNFIELD WITH CYPRESSES

Let me make no bones about 'A Cornfield with Cypresses' –
Make clear straightaway who I am.
I am the painter's mother.
I am old, frail, quivering on my pins,
My trees almost leafless
Being stripped into senility.
But I have still got enough leaves to be able to see
My son's picture for what it is –
The serenest canvas I have ever seen.
(That's saying something
Because my son painted a great many
Serene canvases.)

So why am I so hot under the bra?
(Yes, the bra, I still wear bras
For old times' sake. I am old fashioned.)
I am sore and vexed because the art historian says
That Vincent's 'A Cornfield with Cypresses'
Is evidence of an unbalanced mind.
Poppycock.
Oh I am sure that the art historian
Is a nice little man somewhere
In the lobes of Hampstead
Tending his own poppies, tending his own cocks.
But I do wish that he would look at my son's picture.
Is that too much to ask?
That the art historian might – might – might – might – might
Look at the picture?

I am Vincent's mother
Come to heal the wounds of art history
So smile a little and let me touch you
And as you gaze into the cornfield
You will find yourself
At the heart of the megalotropolis of London
Sitting still and being calm and seeing
In the skies – as my son saw in the skies –
The soul of tiger.
If you look long enough you might even hear a fieldmouse
Piping: Nought sad about death.

TIGER IN A TROPICAL STORM

In the tea room of the old people's home
– Old flame trees, sedges –
– Old tigers not shrinking to put a tooth in it –
In the lit-up dark of a Sunday afternoon in November
I crouch before the broad pointed leaves
Of – I forget what you call it –
Can you remember what you call it? –
Poinsettia! –
I have a visitor, my nephew.
Delighted to see him. Terrified to see him.
He's so young. He's about fifty.
I'm eighty-six, I think.
I bet you he has a lover.
It's written all over him.
I don't have a lover. That's why
I look extra-terrified, wouldn't you
Look extra-terrified if you were confronted
Unexpectedly in the old people's home
By your fifty-year-old
Smiling nephew?

Tiger in a Tropical Storm
Henri Rousseau

I'm healthy. Nothing the matter with me.
I'm as truculent a tiger
As ever I was, burning to go.
My mate got knocked down by a golf ball
(We had a mobile home in the jungle
Adjacent to Godalming)
And I was dumped into the old people's home.
My nephew terrifies me also because of his obvious
Pity for me – his incurable condescension.
I get into a fluster, into a panic.
My tail gets all snarled up
In the legs of my chair.
He whispers (why does he whisper?):
Auntie Tiger, you do not
Look in the least bit absurd.

Why does he say that?
It's because I do look absurd.
As we sit here on the stormy edge of the jungle
Sipping black tea and hissing
We are surrounded by hundreds of other creatures
In slippers, walking-frames, hearing-aids,
The whole zoological gardens quaking.

I am catatonic – can't hide it – that my nephew
Has come to visit his eighty-six-year-old Auntie Tiger
On a Sunday afternoon in November.
He always loved tigers.
Ever since he was a nicens little boy
He had a thing about tigers.
'Because you bite' he used say.
Now he says: Let me touch your stripes.
Who does he think I am – Our Lady of Walsingham?
Waltz with me, nephew, waltz with me.
When he is leaving,
When nobody is looking,
When the nurses are too busy
Nudging all the other tigers back into their cages
He says: May I hold your tail?
I let him. In fact, I wholly intend
To leave him my tail in my will.
He's too mannerly a nephew
To raise the subject of my will and to say:
Give me your tail.
But I will.
In my will I will give you my tail.

Stop. Let me give you my exact address again before you go.
You never know when we might meet again.
We might never meet again.
Jardin des Plantes, Godalming, England, Europe,
The World, The Cosmos.
If you have a lover don't let go of her.
Tigers can be so stupid –
Never see what's right in front of their teeth.

An Old Woman with a Rosary
Paul Cézanne

AN OLD WOMAN WITH A ROSARY

I feel, therefore I am.

Staring down at the dormant face of the rape victim
Is there anyone down there,
Anyone down there at all?

Men take it in turns to taunt her
But she will not look up. 'Cunt!'
They yelp at her but she will not look up.

Us – the lookers on – the chosen johns – the cultured dukes:
Would any of us have the neck – the broken neck –
In public to clutch a pair of rosary beads?

It is for the mysteries of her hands that God made her
And it is for God that the mysteries of her hands pray:
These sawn-off hands of hers that once were

Fingers skimming the keys of winter trees
On the brink of spring. Now all their squirrels gone.
I am your dead mother, clutching my soul in my hands.

Lord Ribblesdale
John Singer Sargent

LORD RIBBLESDALE

If your first impression of me
Is that I am haughty
I forgive you.
One of life's ironies is life itself –
Like the portrait painter's name, Singer Sargent.
In fact I am shy.
Does not my feminine mouth give me away?
It is the lyrical portrait painter who is autocratic.
He demanded I dress up for you like this
But it is by no means my natural drag.

What I much prefer to do when I get the chance,
Which is not often given my obligations,
Is to go out into the forest
And to chop wood in the nip;
To throw off my greatcoat,
To tear off my great boots,
To hang my topper on a tree,
To climb out of my pants
And waistcoat and strew
The woodland floor
With twill and suede,
Silk and starch,
Fling away my whip
And unseen by tabloid
Hacks and paparazzi
To stretch my legs;
Oblivious of all petty members
To sit naked on a fallen bough
And cry my eyes out for my lost sons,

For my lost wife;
To stand naked with an axe
And smile to behold
The finite folly of my Finegan –
My chihuahua Finegan;
To mishit the grain and sprain
My wrist or pull
A muscle in my arm;
Having stared through the trees
At my crumpled gear
To have to crawl on all fours
And with great fear of death
Think of sex,
Pull them all on again,
Think of my ancestors
And me – a naked ostrich
With my root up out of the sand.

As I crawl towards my fallen boot
I mutter to myself:
Ribblesdale, you are a lucky chap.

THE MANTELPIECE

Staring into the marble, I stray into it
Exploring its pores, its veins, its stains, its moles.
A block of marble on legs of marble.
Is it a memorial? An altar?
Am I going to die?
Where is she? Will she ever come back?
Who is she? What is her name?
What kind of a woman

THE MANTELPIECE (LA CHEMINÉE)
Edouard Vuillard

Would have an altar for a mantelpiece?
Would rescue a down-and-out at her gate
And put him to sleep in her own bed?

When she does come back in the late afternoon
She does not speak except to exclaim
'It's May!'
She puts a glass vase of Queen Anne's lace
And daisies on the mantelpiece,
A single poppy, a bramble blossom,
Medicine bottles with labels
Prescribing for me when and how to take them.
She reiterates 'It's May!'
As if she herself is the month of May.
She gives me a book entitled 'Howard's End'.
How does she know that my name is Howard?
She erects a clothes horse
Draping it with white cotton nighties.
I put out a finger with which to trace the marble
But trace her instead – trace her cheekbone.
Is your mantelpiece an altar?
She smiles: Are you my spring lamb?
I am.

That was five and a half years ago.
The world that is the case is everything and new.
O my drowned spring lamb!
O my wild, wild mantelpiece!

PORTRAIT OF GRETA MOLL

Yea my red panther,
My black and green cat,
In her blue cage
In the Jardins des Plantes
Will she meet me tonight
After work?
Come to a movie with me?
Teach me how to live?

My mouth states it all – states of mouth.
Lips that would not kiss you at the point of a pistol
If they chose not to;
Lips that would kiss you into the grave
If they lipped your lips;
Lips that are as self-sufficient as worms,
Yet as reliant as jam;
Lips attuned to society;
Lips addicted to solitude;
Lips with arms.

I am a working woman –
A very different kettle of fish
To that Madame Moitessier in the next room.
Regardez moi! Moi!
Done up to the gills in her finery.
She's not a fish. Not even a kettle.
She's a doll
For middle-aged men to play Balthus with.

Portrait of Greta Moll
Henri Matisse

I am a working woman.
It is not merely for decorum
That I have my sleeves rolled up,
My hair tied up;
That I wear a serviceable blouse;
That I fit into a tight skirt,
My tummy no matter.

I am a working woman
With a studio of my own,
A room with a stove.
When I come home
In the evening I fling
My things on the floor,
Put on Nina Simone,
Curl up on the wall
With my man and
If he's a good boy,
Tall, thin, tender,
Teach him a thing or two,
Theology, ecumenics, Hebrew,
Oh yes, and be taught
By him too –
Currency relations, monetary union,
John Maynard Keynes, Adam Smith.

As I recline on the edge of the motorway
After midnight with my head
The wrong side of the yellow margin
On the hard shoulder,
A pint bottle of vodka in my tummy,
I am not troubled by men
In their toy cars racing past
Who might or might not behead me.
I put my right hand in my left hand
And adjusting my hips
Gaze almond-eyed at the stars
Reading their Arabic from right to left,
Orion, the Plough, the Pleiades,
Feeling self-contained.
I am dear – dear to myself –
Dear Greta Moll.

WOMAN WASHING A PIG

I

I am the pig
Mucking about in the vestibule of the National Gallery
Nosing the mosaic floor.
Eyeball to eyeball with Woolf,
Snout to snout with Churchill,
Trotter to trotter with Fonteyn,
Eliot, Garbo, Sitwells,
Shedding nostril hairs in their crannies,
Depositing forensic evidence
Among the great.

To be a mosaicist
Or a pig
All you have to do
Is to do it
And to do it in the margins
If it's margins that grab you.

The National Gallery pig –
I trot the mosaic floor
Having the best of both worlds
Which is how it should always be.
The most odious ideology
Is the ideology of having one's cake
And not eating it.

Woman Washing a Pig
Boris Anrep

Who in his bladder of bladders,
In her udder of udders,
Would not rather their portrait done
On floor than on wall?
To look down, not up
At one's portrait;
To look down
Like birds like beasts;
The human animal.

'A facetious twentieth-century addition' –
Former assistant keeper Homan Potterton's
Assessment of the mosaic floor.
Facetious, Homan, facetious?
If these mosaics be facetious, Homan,
Then all the world's a Potterton
And all the people in it merely pot boilers.
Which may be the case
But if it is, so what? Not bad.
The mosaic floor is bits of life,
Bits of Pottertons, millions of 'em.

II

We were having Sunday lunch in a hotel by the sea
When I went missing. I was five years old.
My parents had reason to be worried.
Many people had been drowned in that sea.
The perimeter of the hotel ran along a cliff.
I heard the hue and cry go up.
My name being called – Paul, Paul.
But I was content where I was
Sitting up in the pig sty with the sow
Among a dozen piglets or *bonnavs*
As Daddy had always lovingly called them.
I loved when he spoke lovingly
And he never spoke more lovingly
Than when he spoke Irish.

I was up to my waist and elbows
In muck and when they found me
I wanted to stay where I was.
I squealed to be let forage with the pigs.
Daddy wanted to beat me there and then
But Mummy said I should first be washed.
As she was the one who at home
Always washed the family pig
It was a trauma familiar to her
To wash me and with her bare hands
Wipe the pig shit off me.

By the time she had talced and towelled me
The mood for a thrashing had left Daddy
And he settled for a lecture on the fundamental
Baseness of little boys, the fundamental
Baseness of swine and how if he ever
Caught me in a pig sty again
He'd trample me to death with his own feet.

III

In my pig sty in Trafalgar Square
At twilight
I lie down on the floor.
I let thousands of visitors
From all over London and the world
Walk over me.
Lying down with my pig
I get walked on, stood on,
Stamped on, trampled on.
There is nothing like getting walked on
To teach you perspective and tone.

Such is the glamour of Soho and Covent Garden,
Of Whitehall and Piccadilly,
That when in old age
My poor pink pig
In exits and entrances
Curls up in pools of her own pee
There is no one to wash her
Except me – the woman downstairs.
I whom even still
In the tail-end of the twentieth century
You persist in denying:
In the Grand Circle entrance
Of this evening's matinée performance
Of *Me and My Girl*;
Or tonight in the side entrance to the stalls
Of *Dancing At Lughnasa*.

What I love about my pig,
What I respect and admire her for,
Is that she is always
Putting her foot in it.
Forever putting her trotter
Into the wrong conversation.
I wheel my pig in my pram
Into the pub behind the National Gallery
Only to be told at the bar
– The bar tiered with pint-drinking yuppies –
'We don't serve pigs.'

I revere my pig also for her bust:
There is nothing more edifying than tens of thousands of tits.

But we do get served in Clapham Common,
In the North Pole in Clapham Common.
We sit in the North Pole
For the night sipping bitter,
Mulling over fifty years in London.
Me and my pig
Have lived all over the shop:
Powis Terrace, Cranley Gardens, Great Percy Street,
Sydney Street, Gloucester Road, Queen's Gate,
Buckingham Palace Gate, Brixton, Catford,
Ladbroke Grove where in the Kensington Park Hotel
I washed my pig every night and no one complained.
In Holloway I lived with my pig
In a basement;
In Bayswater I lived with my pig
In a cupboard;
In Wood Green I lived with my pig
In a TV repair shop;
In Lambeth I lived with my pig
In the house where Charlie Chaplin was born
In West Square.

London has been good to me and my pig.
Only the beauties with bombs get on my nerves.
Them with their dual nationality.
For sanity I repair to Muriel's.
O to be in Muriel's now that winter's here.
With Francis, Lucien, Paul Potts, Michael;
Washing the pig in Muriel's.

When I am not washing the pig
I am nursing the piglet
Upside down in my arms
And when I am not nursing the piglet
I am carrying the can –
That glorified milkpail
Belovèd of poets.
Poets also get on my nerves.
Poets are so full of themselves,
Empty of others.

Ah, but our London days!
Before them our Berlin days
Messing about with the painters
In *The Black Piglet* café;
Francis with his own chauffeur,
Lighting his cigars with Deutschmarks.

The day has almost ended.
Monastic choirs of warders
Are dragnetting
The galleries of the western world,
All garnering for evensong
In the great vestibule
Where I lie down with my own,
My Pig Reclining.
Shag all. Shag all.

Woman being woman;
Not tied to Tom;
Not necessarily tied to Tom;
Woman washing the pig.

LEISURE

I

Scared as I am of a Tom on the wall
I would be infinitely more scared
Of a Wystan on the wall.
Hug a shady wet nun!

II

I love lying up in Loch Ness
The whole day long
Doing nothing,
Just scrutinizing my wife's breasts,
Pondering the 2.30 at Ayr.

LEISURE
Boris Anrep

III

Questions and answers.
Funny things.
If there were answers
There would be no questions.
How could there be?
$E = MC^2$

IV

Einstein, is it the case with the world
That the Loch Ness Monster, my wife and I
Are all one and the same person?
Not to mention my father?

V

In the bosom of the monster
Lying facedown on a balustrade overlooking Ness
I who carry the century in my slippers.
Much painting to be done, much sculpting,
Much sitting down in the Regency armchair,
Much getting to know the corner of Einstein's Field.

VI

All shall be well
And all manner of thing shall be well
When leisure is the basis of culture
And the novelist wakes up without her husband
Nagging at her to scratch his back or console his coccyx
And the education adds up:
In the name of the mother, the daughter, and the holy spirit.

Crivelli's Garden
Paula Rego

CRIVELLI'S GARDEN

O my mother
You are water –
The sole subject matter;
My piece of blue.
To which owl
Is sentinel
As well as to the null
To the full
Moon over Big Ben.

I

I am the man in your life,
The little man in your life.

My littleness is what I have to offer.
It is for my littleness that you woo me.

Belittle me.
I will go on being little.

Go on being ink in a ménage of blood and offal.
Go on being sepia in a blue-and-white ménage.

You confide: An affectionate little fellow –
My little Baptist with his little lamb.

II

From where I stand and loiter and keep vigil
On the wall of the Sainsbury Wing Restaurant
What a marvellous point of view!
Red buses, black cabs, fountains, lions,
Pilgrims with rucksacks, umbrellas, briefcases
And when I have had my fill of Trafalgar Square
Or of faces full of knives and forks
I turn my head to Paula's Wall and, laughing, weep:

For mother to hold me in her hands again
And dip me in the fountain,
Introduce me to water,
My face to reflectiveness.

As once on the side of the road home
From London to Hereford
On chips of blue-and-white road metal
We stopped to picnic
And listened to Granny
Telling stories with her thick black legs wide apart.
After you Mother
It was Grandmother
Who seduced me
And revealed to me the possibilities of the world.

III

For mother to come again
Sweeping the floor of the world;
For mother – long dead in Hereford –
To beetle round the corner of the Strand,
Round the date tree of St Martin-in-the-Fields,
With her toad-dragon in tow on a leash,
To meet her cronies in the railway station.
She snaps: 'I am staying in the Charing Cross Hotel
In a poky little room with a large bathroom.
I like poky little rooms with large bathrooms.
You get a nice sort of person staying there.
I had breakfast this morning in the Betjeman Restaurant
With a young man in black who told me
That his name was Simon Armitage.
Such marvellous names people have nowadays.
In the Pilgrim's Bar last night
The young woman next me told me
That her name was Tess Gallagher.
She had a drawing book with crayons and pencils.
She exclaimed: I have crossed over London Bridge.
I identified with her. My own late husband
Had a passion for London Bridge.'

Mother speaking with her hand over her mouth.
I hate when she does that.
Although she is probably not saying
What I think she is saying.
No, she is not talking about you, son.
Mothers have preoccupations other than men.
She is confiding in Elizabeth
The pain of pre-menstrual tension.
O Lord, it is no joke being a man
With all these orifices, cavities.
I have to go to the doctor tomorrow
To get my earhole washed out.
But can you imagine – can you –
What it must be like to be a woman?

I am the only man here in my bare feet.
I am the only man here.

INDEX

8.
The Marriage of the Virgin
Niccolò di Buonaccorso (active 1372–88)
egg tempera on wood
51 × 33 cm

10.
Giovanni Arnolfini (?) and his Wife Giovanna Cenami (?) (The Arnolfini Marriage)
Jan van Eyck (active 1422–41)
oil, perhaps with some egg tempera, on oak
81.8 × 59.7 cm

12.
An Unidentified Scene
Domenico Beccafumi (1486(?)–1551)
oil on wood
74 × 137.8 cm

14.
Apollo and Daphne
Antonio del Pollaiuolo (*c.* 1432–96)
oil on wood
29.5 × 20 cm

16.
The Virgin and Child with Saints Anthony Abbot and George
Pisanello (active 1395–1455(?))
egg tempera on poplar
47 × 29.2 cm

20.
Saint John the Baptist Retiring to the Desert
Giovanni di Paolo (active 1420–82)
egg tempera on poplar
31.1 × 38.8 cm

22.
The Presentation in the Temple
The Master of the Life of the Virgin (active second half of the fifteenth century)
oil on oak
84 × 108.5 cm

24.
Portrait of a Lady in Yellow
Alesso Baldovinetti (c. 1426–99)
wood
62.9 × 40.6 cm

28.
Samson and Delilah
Andrea Mantegna (*c.* 1430/31–1506)
glue size on linen
47 × 36.8 cm

32.
Charlemagne and the Meeting of Saints Joachim and Ann
Studio of the Master of Moulins (active *c.* 1483–1500)
wood, a fragment
71.8 × 59.1 cm

34.
Saints Peter and Dorothy
The Master of the Saint Bartholomew Altarpiece (active *c.* 1470–1510)
oil on oak
125.7 × 71.1 cm

36.
The Adoration of the Kings
Jan Gossaert, sometimes called Mabuse (active 1503–32)
oil on oak
177.2 × 161.3 cm

44.
Portrait of a Young Man
Andrea del Sarto (1486–1530)
oil on linen
72.4 × 57.2 cm

46.
Cupid Complaining to Venus
Lucas Cranach the Elder (1472–1553)
oil transferred from wood to synthetic panel
81.3 × 54.6 cm

50.
Portrait of a Man
Parmigianino (1503–40)
oil on wood
89.5 × 63.8 cm

52.
Portrait of Susanna Lunden(?) (Le Chapeau de Paille)
Peter Paul Rubens (1577–1640)
oil on oak
79 × 54 cm

56.
A Lady with a Squirrel and a Starling
Hans Holbein the Younger (1497/98–1543)
oil on oak
56 × 38.8 cm

58.
The Death of Actaeon
Titian (1511–76)
oil on canvas
178.4 × 198.1 cm

63.
The Supper at Emmaus
Michelangelo Merisi da Caravaggio (1573–1610)
oil on canvas
141 × 196.2 cm

66.
Christ Appearing to Saint Peter on the Appian Way (Domine Quo Vadis?)
Annibale Carracci (1560–1609)
wood
77.4 × 56.3 cm

68.
Samson and Delilah
Peter Paul Rubens (1577–1640)
oil on oak
185 × 205 cm

72.
Portrait of Govaert van Surpele (?) and His Wife
Jacob Jordaens (1593–1678)
oil on canvas
213.3 × 189 cm

74.
The Grote Kerk, Haarlem
Pieter Saenredam (1597–1665)
oil on oak
59.5 × 81.7 cm

78.
Cardinal Richelieu
Philippe de Champaigne (1602–74)
oil on canvas
259.7 × 177.8 cm

81.
A Family Group in a Landscape
Frans Hals (1580(?)–1666)
oil on canvas
148.5 × 251 cm

84.
The Toilet of Venus (The Rokeby Venus)
Diego Velázquez (1599–1660)
oil on canvas
122.5 × 177 cm

86.
The Annunciation
Nicolas Poussin (1594(?)–1665)
oil on canvas
104.8 × 102.9 cm

88.
A Sleeping Maid and Her Mistress
Nicolaes Maes (1634–93)
oil on oak
70 × 53.3 cm

90.
River Landscape with Horseman and Peasants
Aelbert Cuyp (1620–91)
oil on canvas
123 × 241 cm

92.
The Rest on the Flight into Egypt
Adriaen van der Werff (1659–1722)
oil on oak
54.5 × 43 cm

95.

Mr and Mrs Andrews

Thomas Gainsborough (1722–88)

oil on canvas

69.8 × 119.4 cm

98.

Exhibition of a Rhinoceros at Venice

Pietro Longhi (1702(?)–85)

oil on canvas

60.4 × 47 cm

100.

The Painter's Daughters Chasing a Butterfly

Thomas Gainsborough (1722–88)

oil on canvas

113.5 × 105 cm

104.

Mr and Mrs Thomas Coltman

Joseph Wright of Derby (1734–97)

oil on canvas

127 × 101.6 cm

110.

Madame de Pompadour

François-Hubert Drouais (1727–75)

oil on canvas

217 × 156.8 cm

112.
General Sir Banastre Tarleton
Joshua Reynolds (1723–92)
oil on canvas
236 × 145.5 cm

116.
Young Ladies on the Bank of the Seine
Jean-Désiré-Gustave Courbet (1819–77)
canvas
96.5 × 130 cm

119.
The Stove in the Studio
Paul Cézanne (1839–1906)
oil on canvas
41 × 30 cm

121.
Young Spartans Exercising
Hilaire-Germain-Edgar Degas (1834–1917)
oil on canvas
109.2 × 154.3 cm

126.
Miss La La at the Cirque Fernando
Hilaire-Germain-Edgar Degas (1834–1917)
oil on canvas
116.8 × 77.5 cm

132.
'The Rosy Wealth of June'
Ignace-Henri-Jean-Théodore Fantin-Latour (1836–1904)
oil on canvas
70.5 × 61.6 cm

134.
A Cornfield, with Cypresses
Vincent van Gogh (1853–90)
oil on canvas
72.1 × 90.9 cm

138.
Tiger in a Tropical Storm
Henri Rousseau (1844–1910)
oil on canvas
129.8 × 161.9 cm

142.
An Old Woman with a Rosary
Paul Cézanne (1839–1906)
oil on canvas
80.6 × 65.5 cm

144.
Lord Ribblesdale
John Singer Sargent (1856–1925)
oil on canvas
258.4 × 143.5 cm

147.
The Mantelpiece (La Cheminée)
Edouard Vuillard (1868–1940)
oil on pasteboard
51.4 × 77.5 cm

150.
Portrait of Greta Moll
Henri Matisse (1869–1954)
oil on canvas
93 × 73.5 cm

154.
Woman Washing a Pig
Boris Anrep (1885–1969)
mosaic

162.
Leisure
Boris Anrep (1885–1969)
mosaic

164.
Crivelli's Garden
Paula Rego (b. 1935)
mural